Andrew looked at his watch. It was time to deliver his batch of morning newspapers for *The Star*.

"I am going now,"
Andrew said to his
mom and dad. "See
you back here at nine."

Andrew wheeled his bike
down the back steps.
The morning dew was
still on the grass. A
bird flew to its nest.

Andrew chewed gum and threw papers on each porch. His bike had a rusty chain and dented fenders.

"I can not wait until I
save up for a new bike,"
he said to himself, as
he rode down the street.

Suddenly he heard a click, click, clicking sound. Andrew sighed and said, "What is that?"

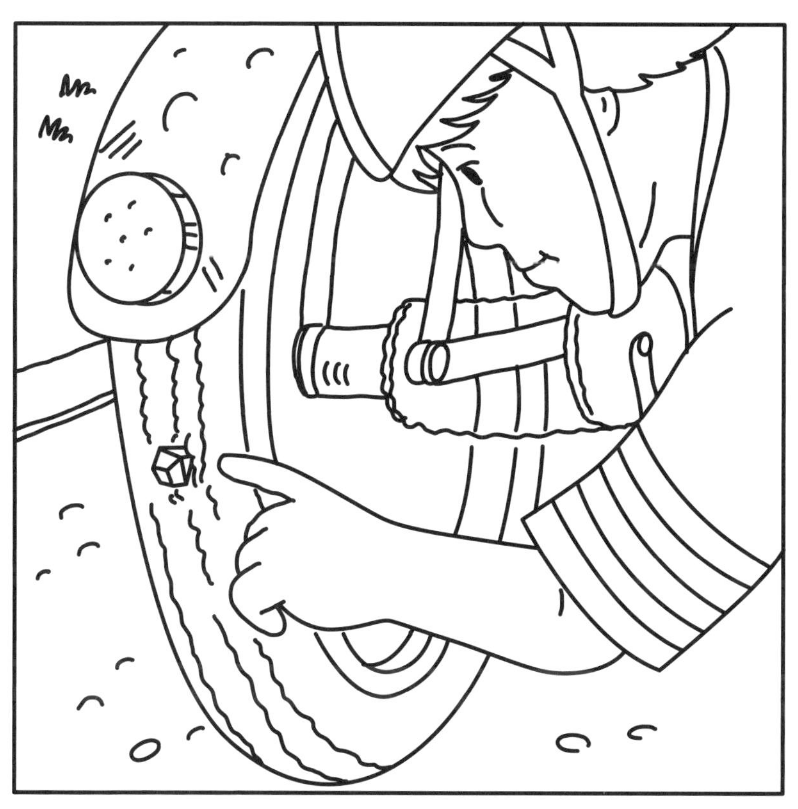

Andrew got off his bike to look at the tires. "I am glad they are not flat," he said. Then he saw a bright stone stuck in one tire. He stuffed it into his pocket.

Andrew had fun finding
things and stuffing
them into his pockets.
He found a new marble
and it went into
his pocket.

8

He found a red clip near
the mailbox. It went into
his pocket.

When he got home,
Andrew took all the stuff
out of his pockets. He
showed his mom and
dad the marble and the
red clip.

"And look," he said,
showing them the stone
he had found. When he
blew off the dirt, the
stone sparkled.

"That looks like a jewel," said his mom.

"Andrew, look at this," said his dad, pointing to a story in the morning newspaper.

"Mrs. Brewster has lost the jewel from her ring," his dad said. "I think you may have found it! She will reward you!"

They went to see
Mrs. Brewster.
Andrew said, "Is this
yours? It was stuck
in my bike tire."

14

"Yes!" she said. "This is the jewel from my ring. I am thrilled! And I want you to take this as a reward."

"Thanks," said Andrew,
"this is my lucky day. Now
I can get a new bike."
Mrs. Brewster said,
"Andrew, thanks to you,
this is my lucky day, too!"